Look and Find®

MARVEL

ANT-MAN

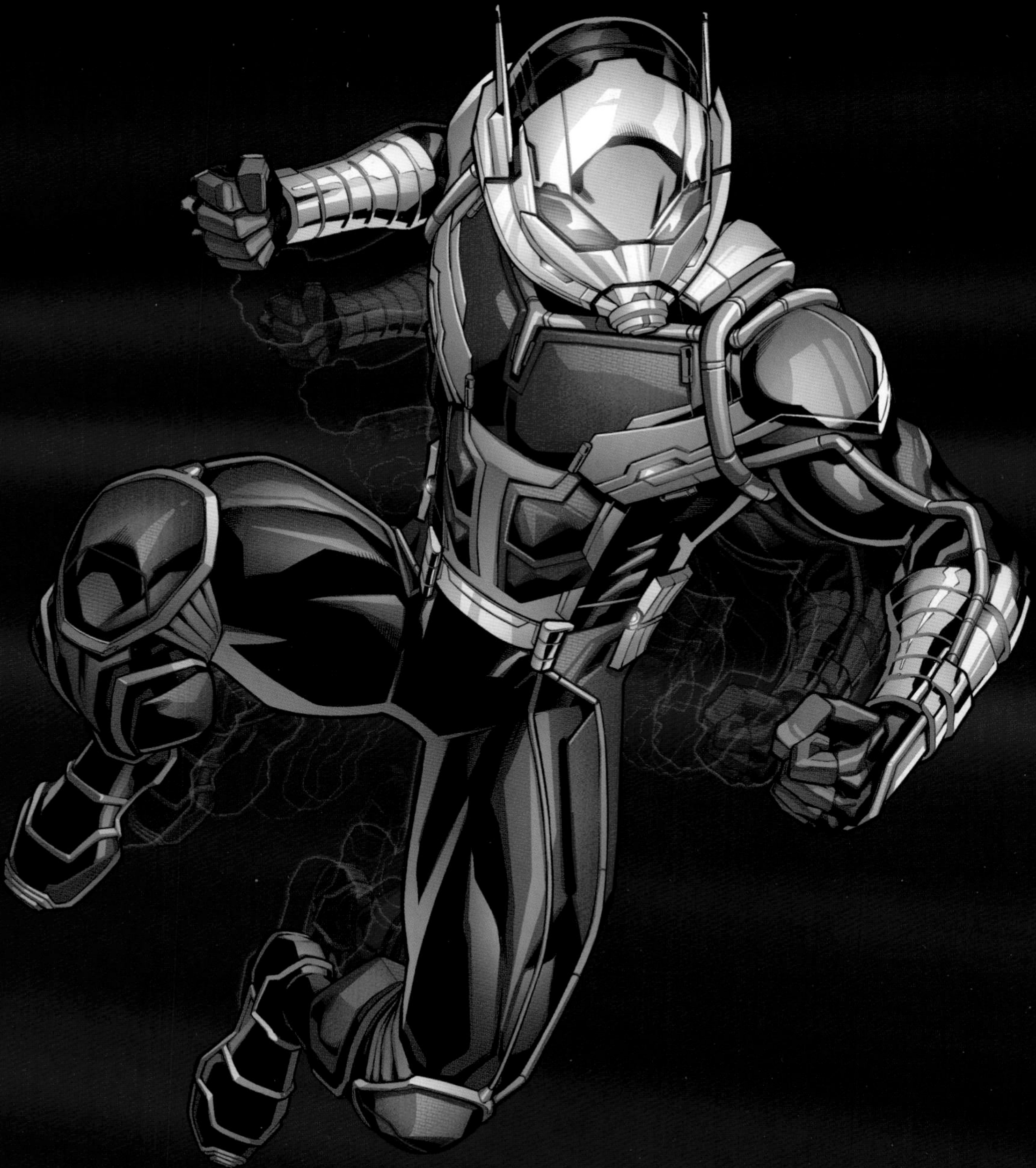

we make books come alive®

Phoenix International Publications, Inc.

Chicago • London • New York • Hamburg • Mexico City • Paris • Sydney

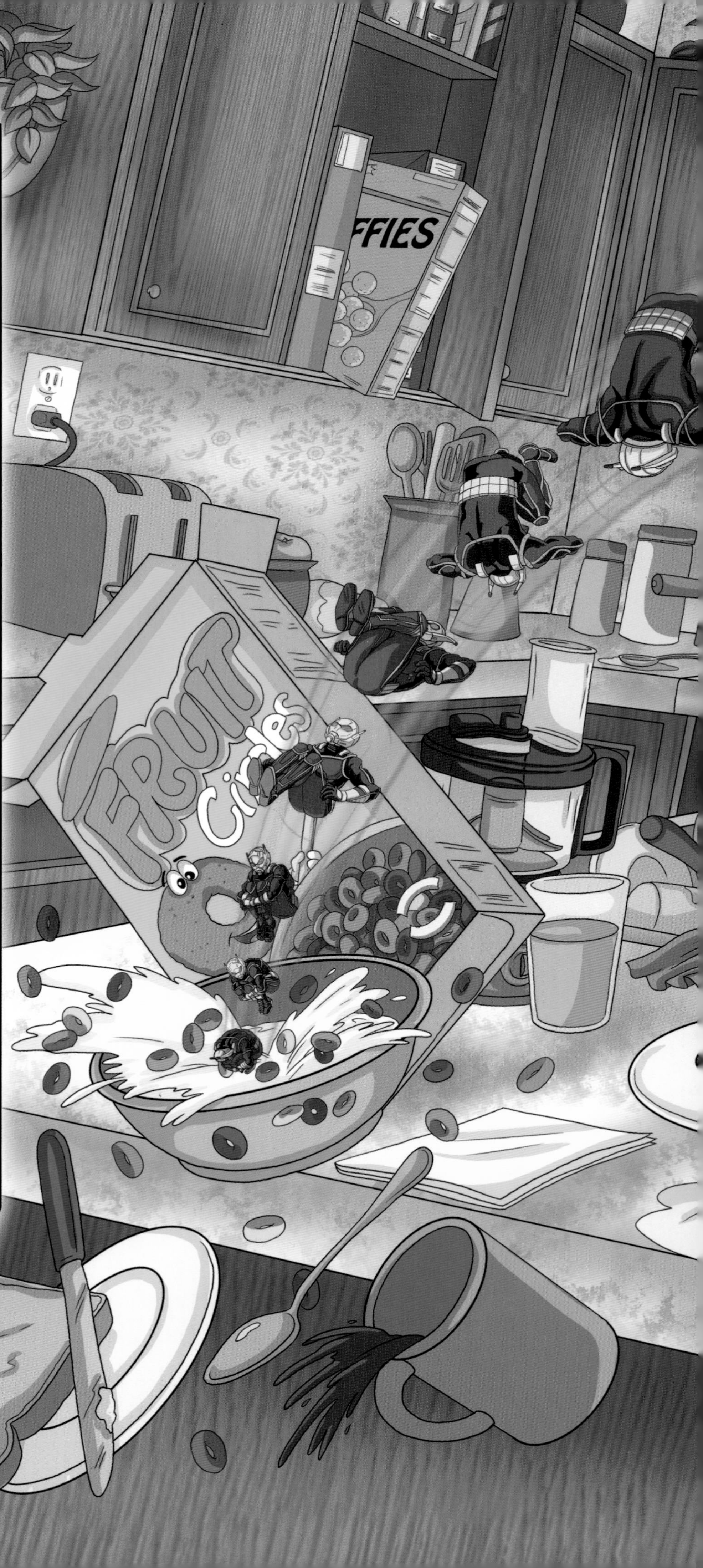
FFIES
FRUIT
Circles

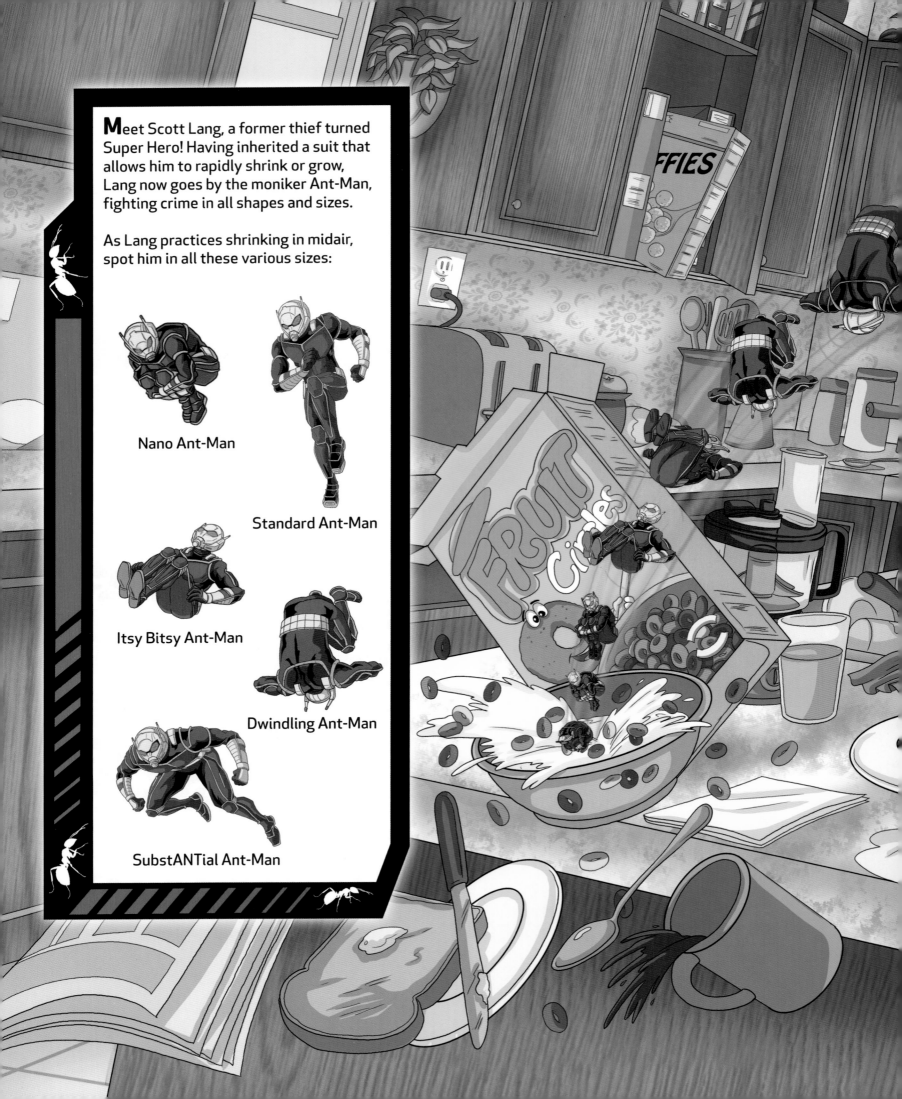

Meet Scott Lang, a former thief turned Super Hero! Having inherited a suit that allows him to rapidly shrink or grow, Lang now goes by the moniker Ant-Man, fighting crime in all shapes and sizes.

As Lang practices shrinking in midair, spot him in all these various sizes:

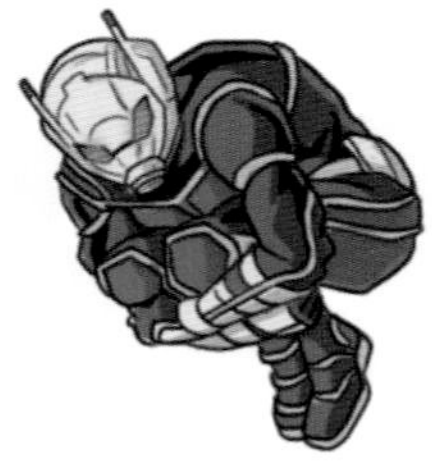

Nano Ant-Man

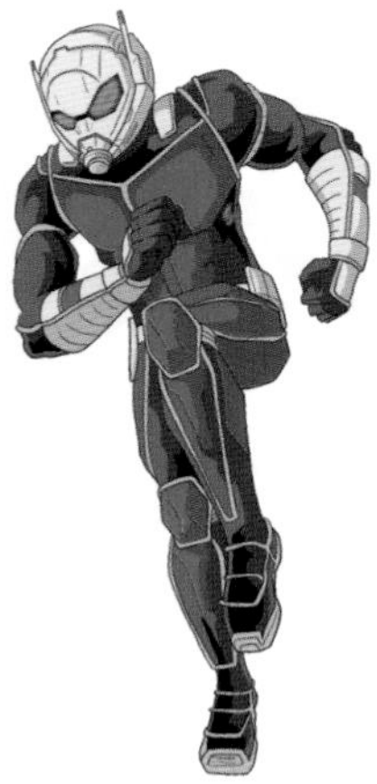

Standard Ant-Man

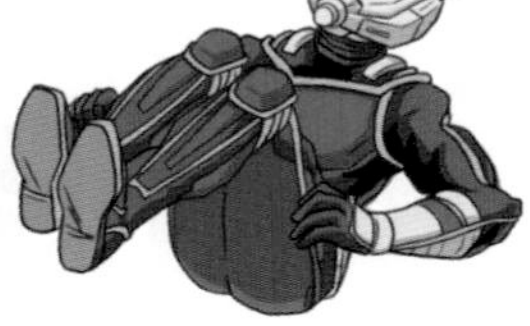

Itsy Bitsy Ant-Man

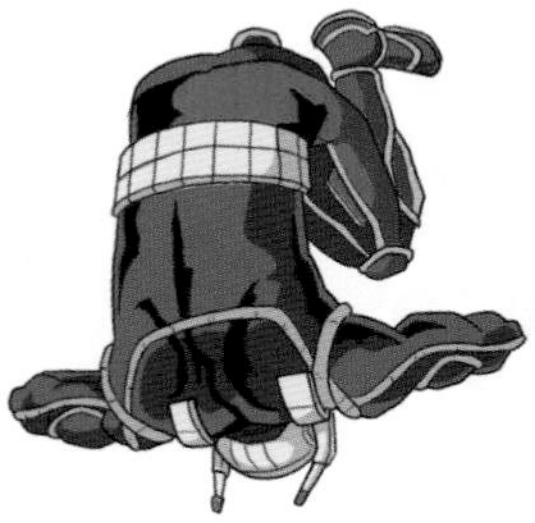

Dwindling Ant-Man

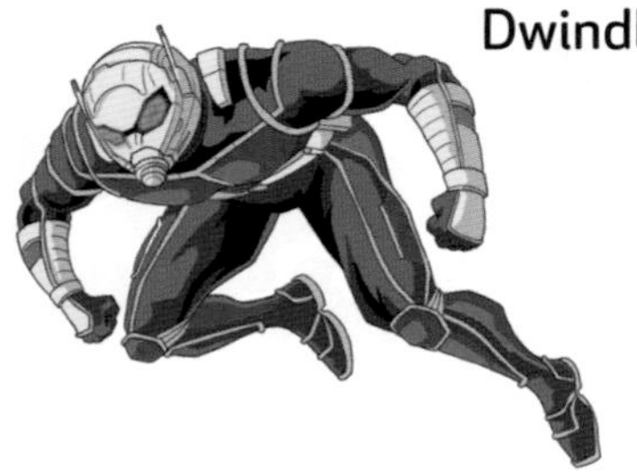

SubstANTial Ant-Man

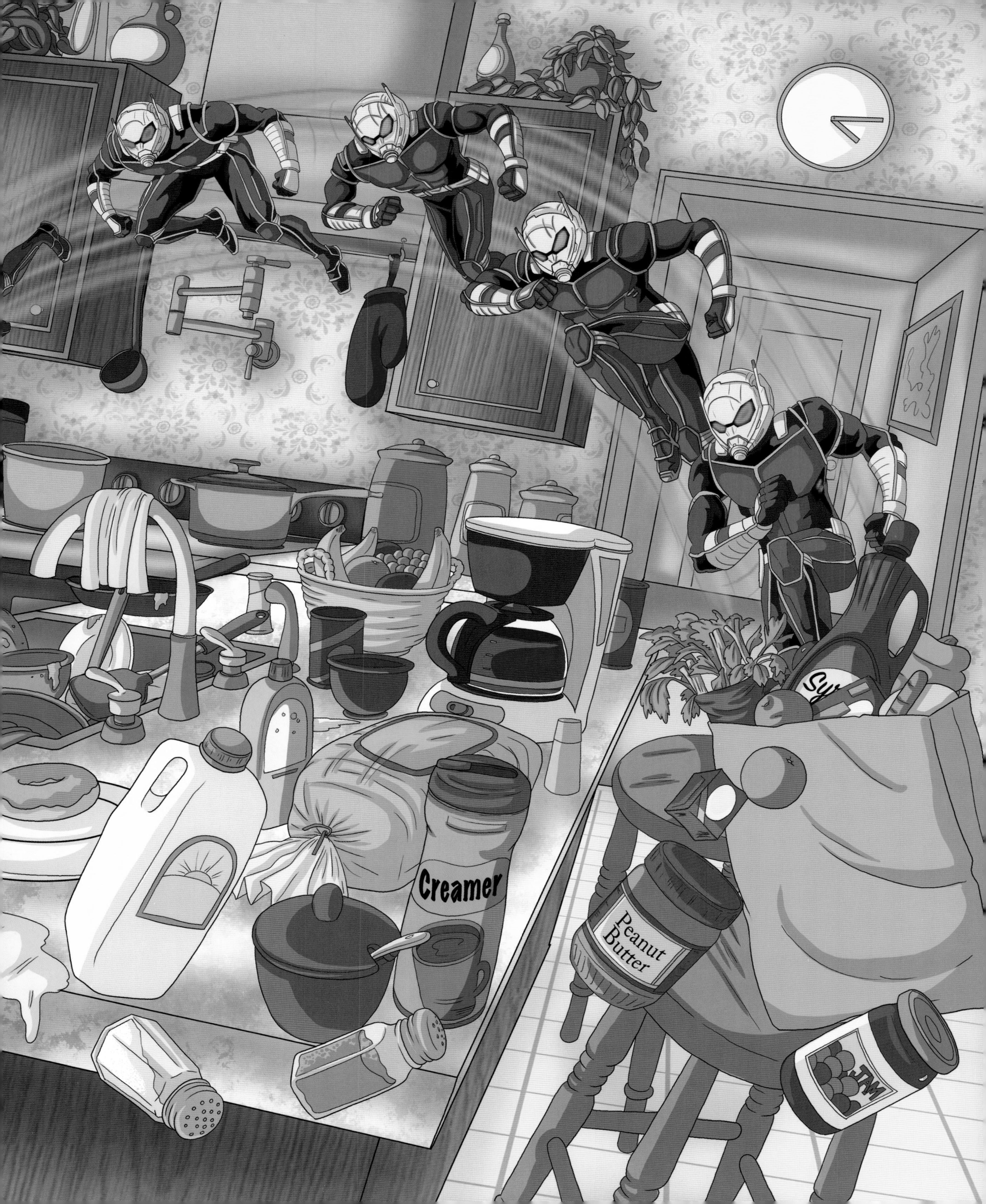
Creamer
Peanut Butter
JAM

Deep in the Swiss mountains, Arnim Zola conspires to defeat the Avengers. Ant-Man and the Wasp sneak into Zola's library, seeking clues in order to stop him.

While Ant-Man and the Wasp stay out of sight, spot these global landmarks:

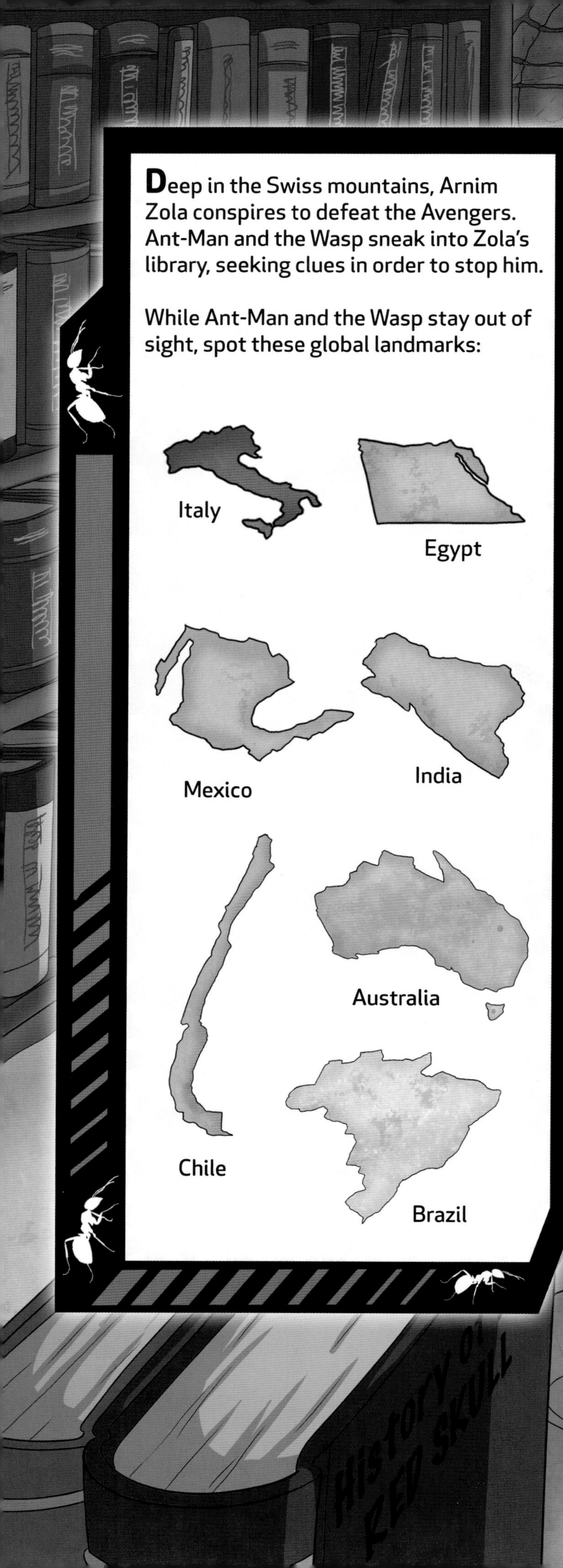
Italy
Egypt
Mexico
India
Chile
Australia
Brazil

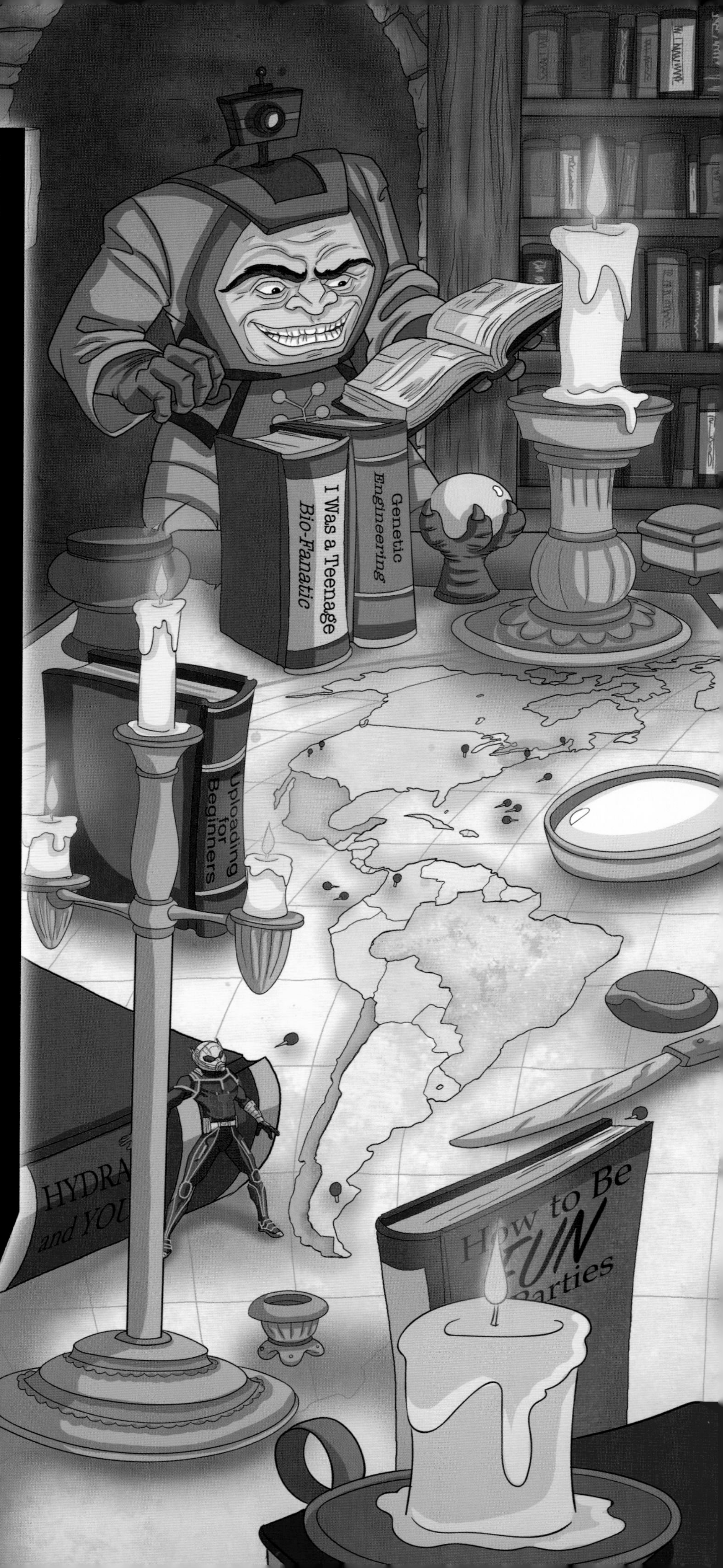
I Was a Teenage Bio-Fanatic
Genetic Engineering
Uploading for Beginners
HYDRA
and YOU
FUN
Parties
History of RED SKULL

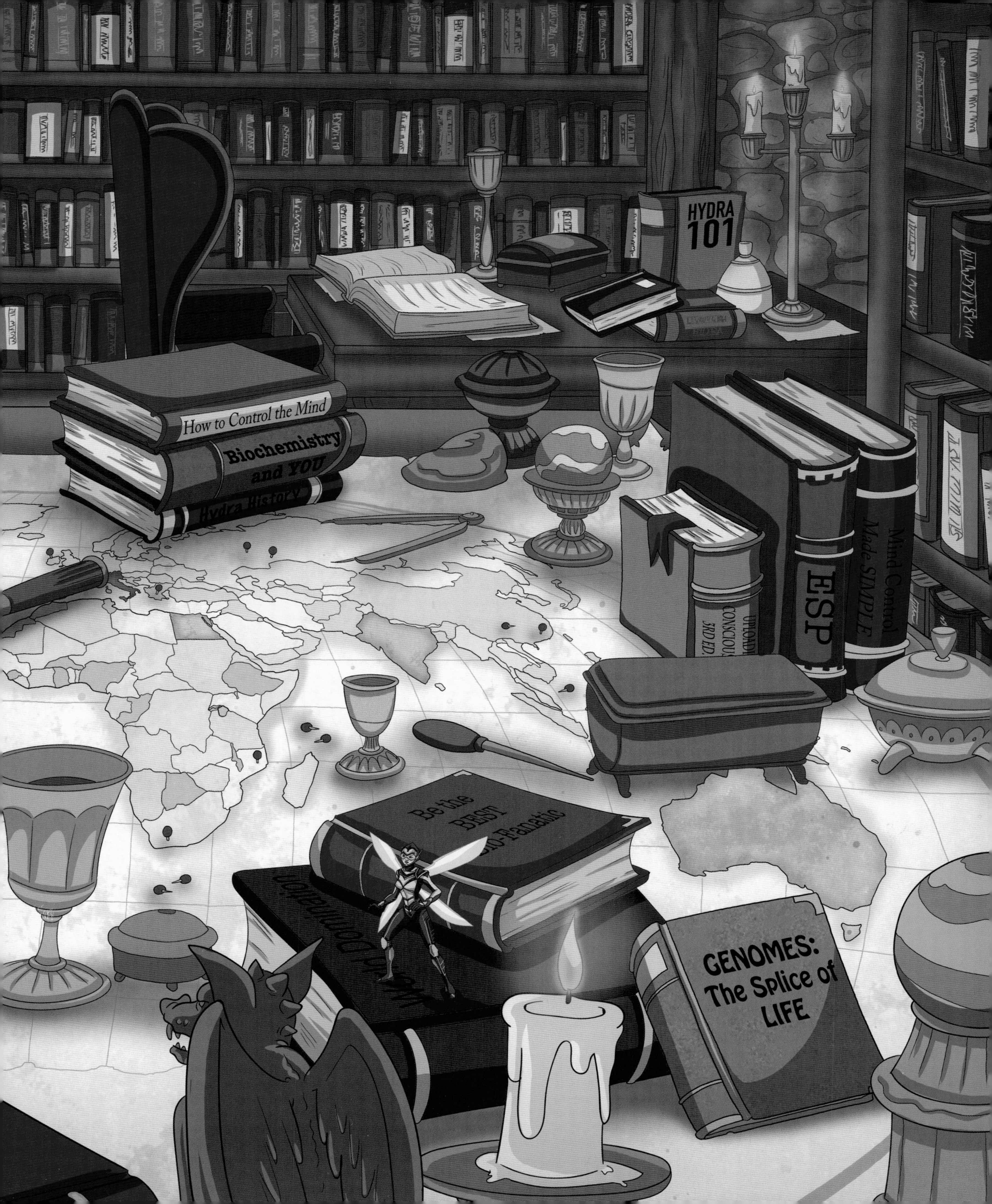
HYDRA 101
How to Control the Mind
Biochemistry and YOU
Hydra History
ESP
Mind Control Made SIMPLE
Be the BEST
GENOMES: The Splice of LIFE

Taskmaster has the uncanny ability to replicate every movement he sees—including Ant-Man's! Since Ant-Man and the Wasp can't outfight Taskmaster, they will have to outnumber him instead.

Find these intrepid insects Ant-Man has recruited for assistance:

ant eating its weight in crumbs

ant sticking to the point

shortsighted ant

ant dropping in

ant eluding arrows

ant catching some Zzzs

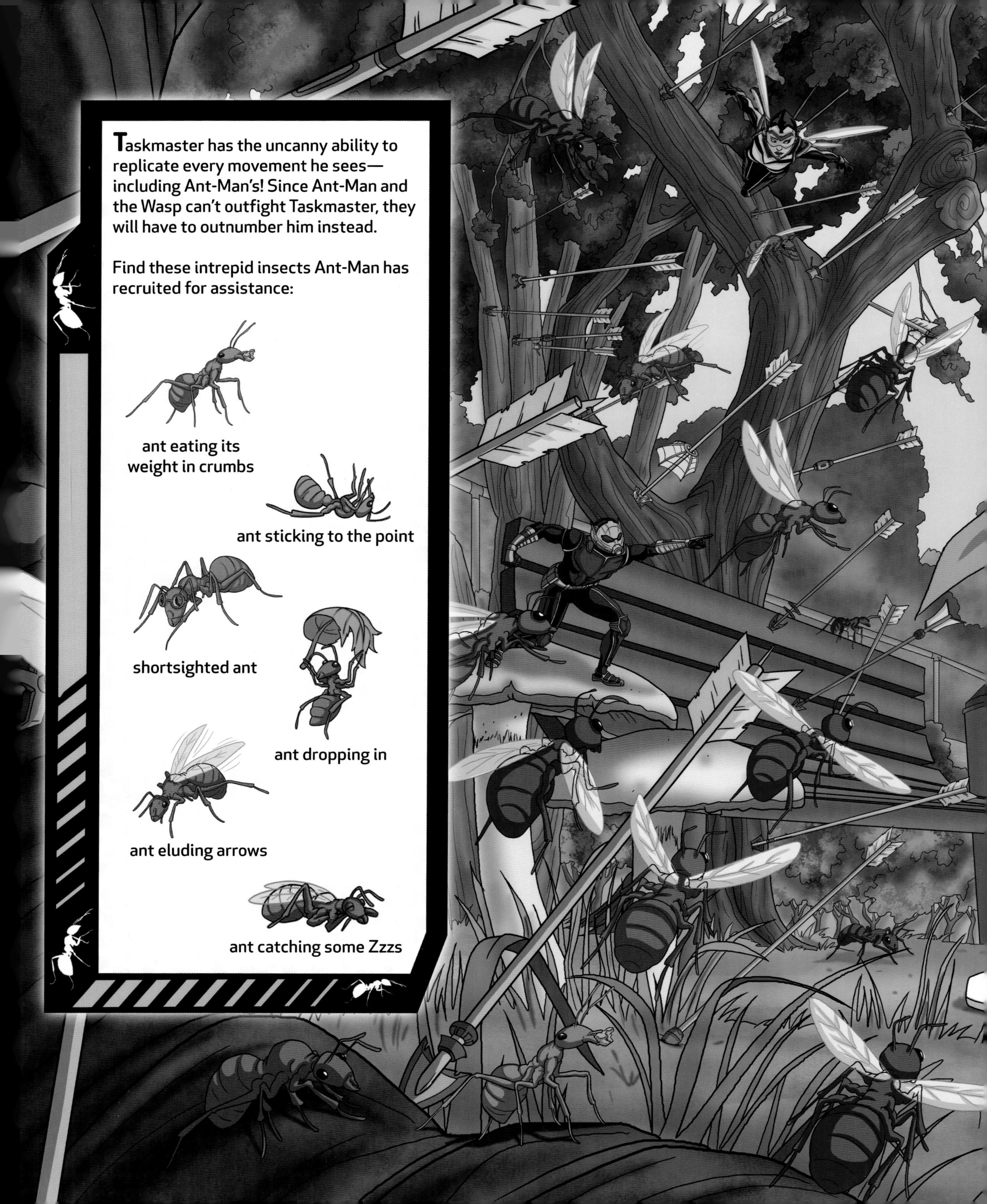

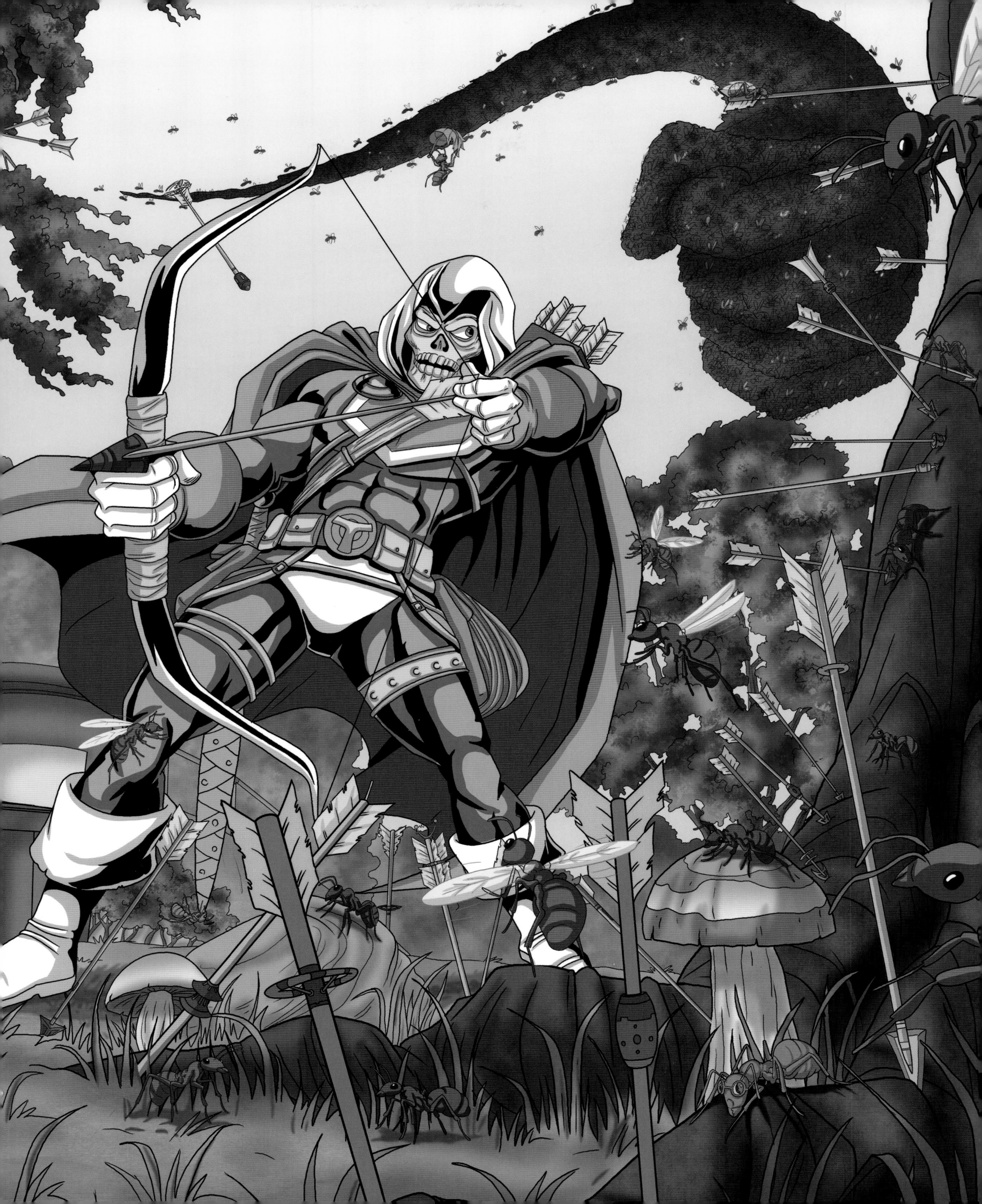

Hydra has used its technology to invent an ultra-magnifying glass! Harnessing the power of the sun, this weapon is capable of zapping Ant-Man and the Wasp for good.

As Ant-Man magni-*flies* out of Hydra's range, find these objects caught in the magnifying glass's cross beams:

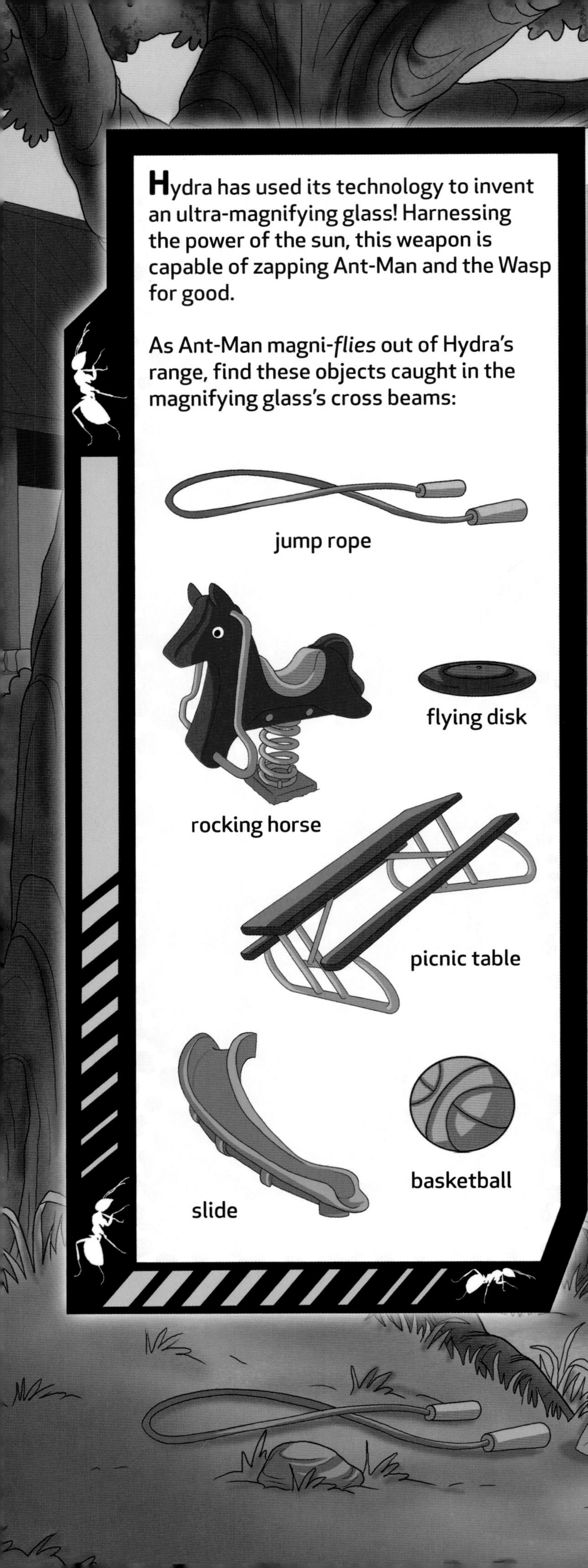

jump rope
rocking horse
flying disk
picnic table
slide
basketball

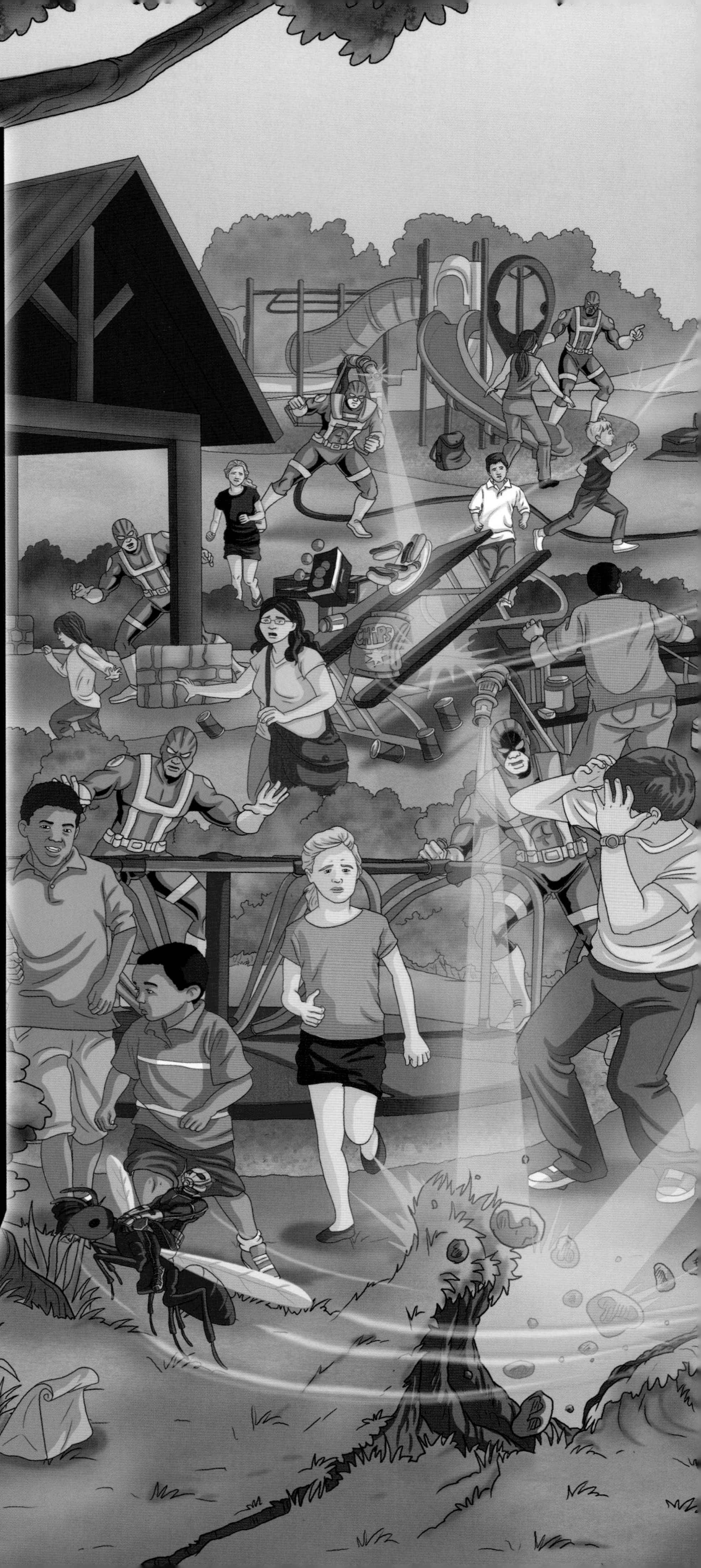

CHIPS

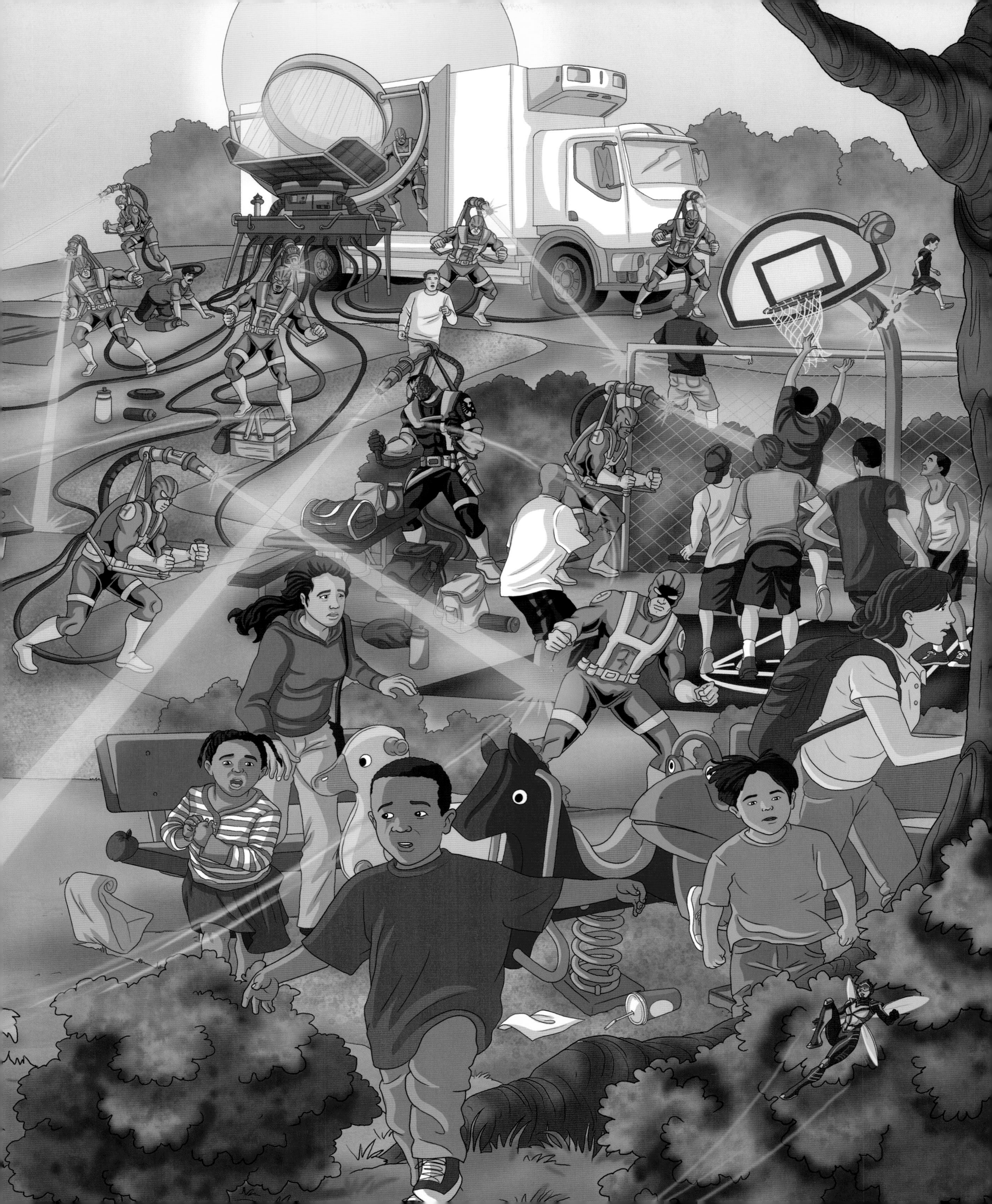

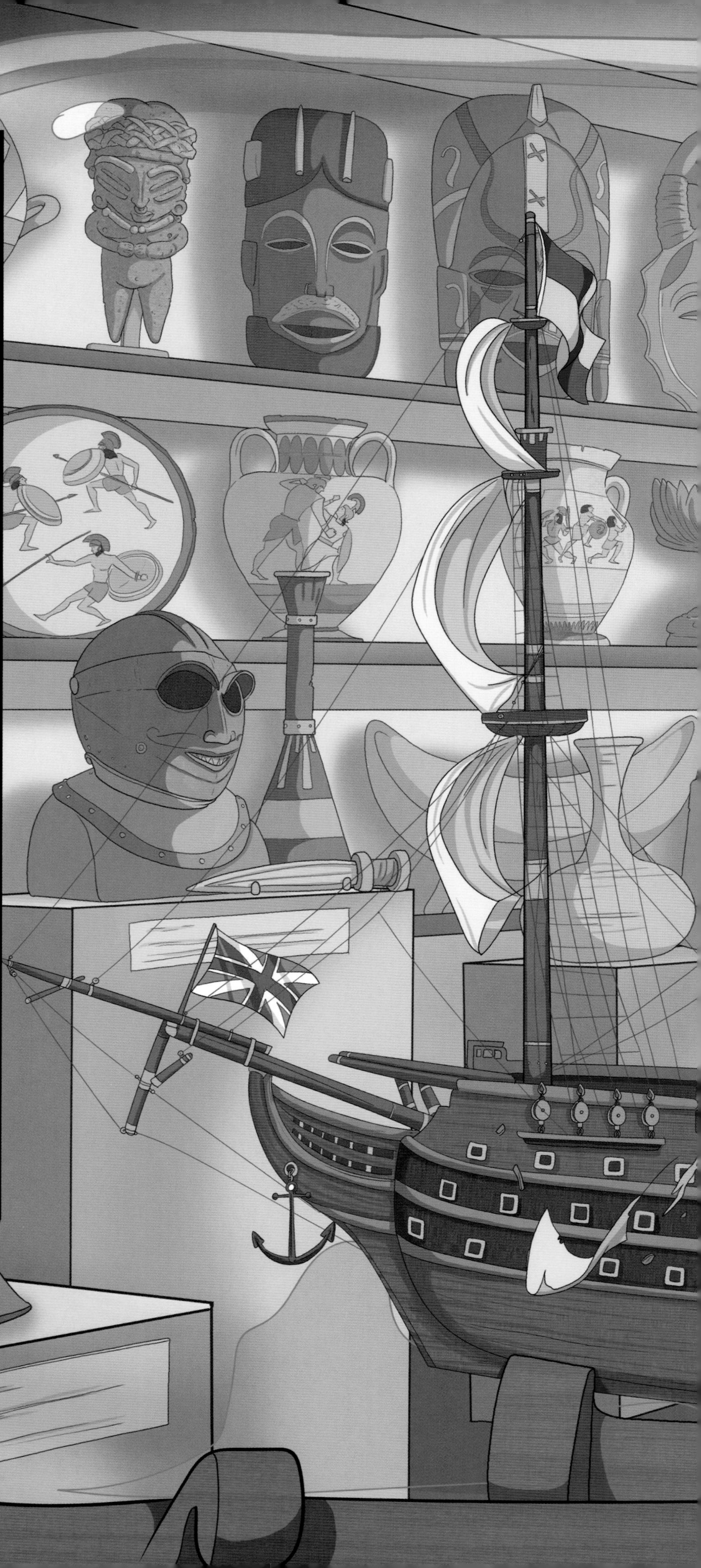

Whirlwind's attempt to rob a history museum is foiled when Ant-Man uses Pym Particles to shrink him down to size. Now they're battling on an unlikely stage!

While Ant-Man hoists the mainsail and Whirlwind walks the plank, spot this ship's miniature models:

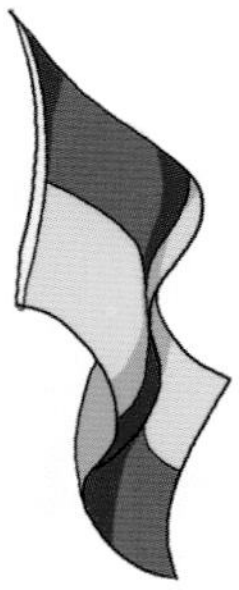

flag

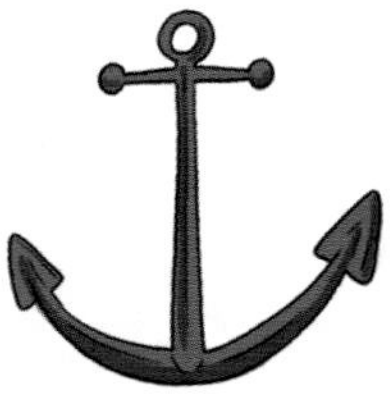

anchor

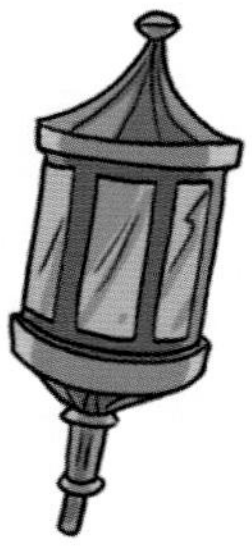

lantern

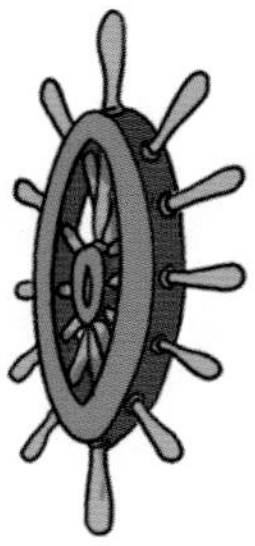

ship's wheel

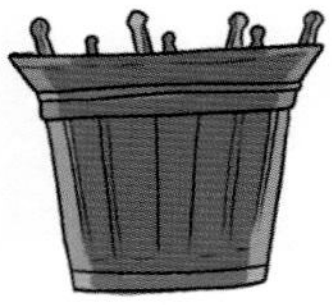

crow's nest

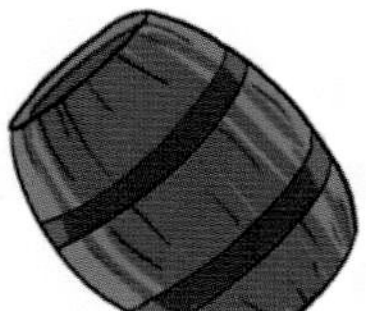

barrel

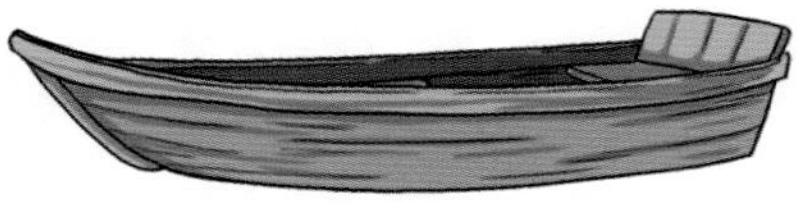

rowboat

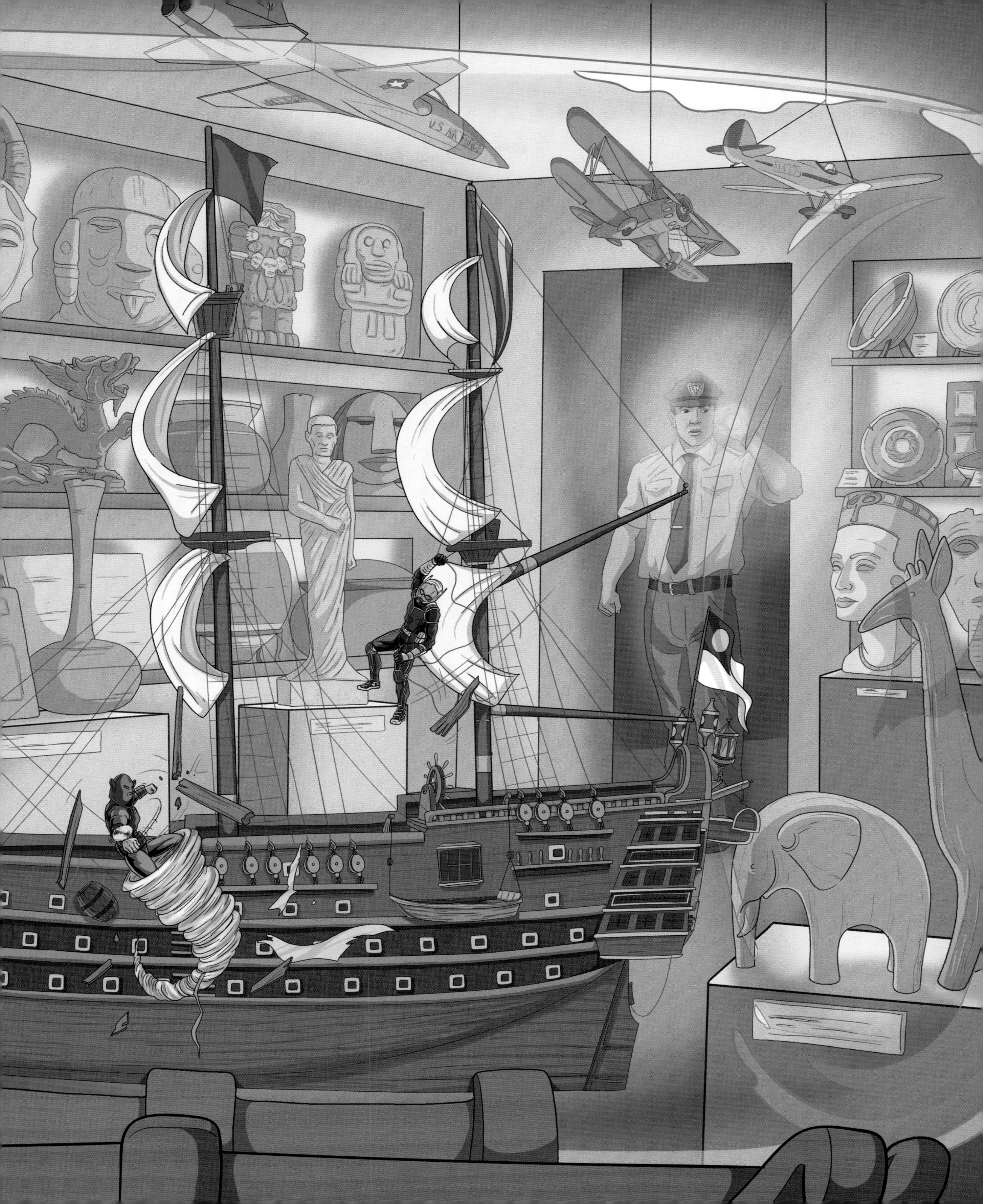
U.S. AIR FORCE

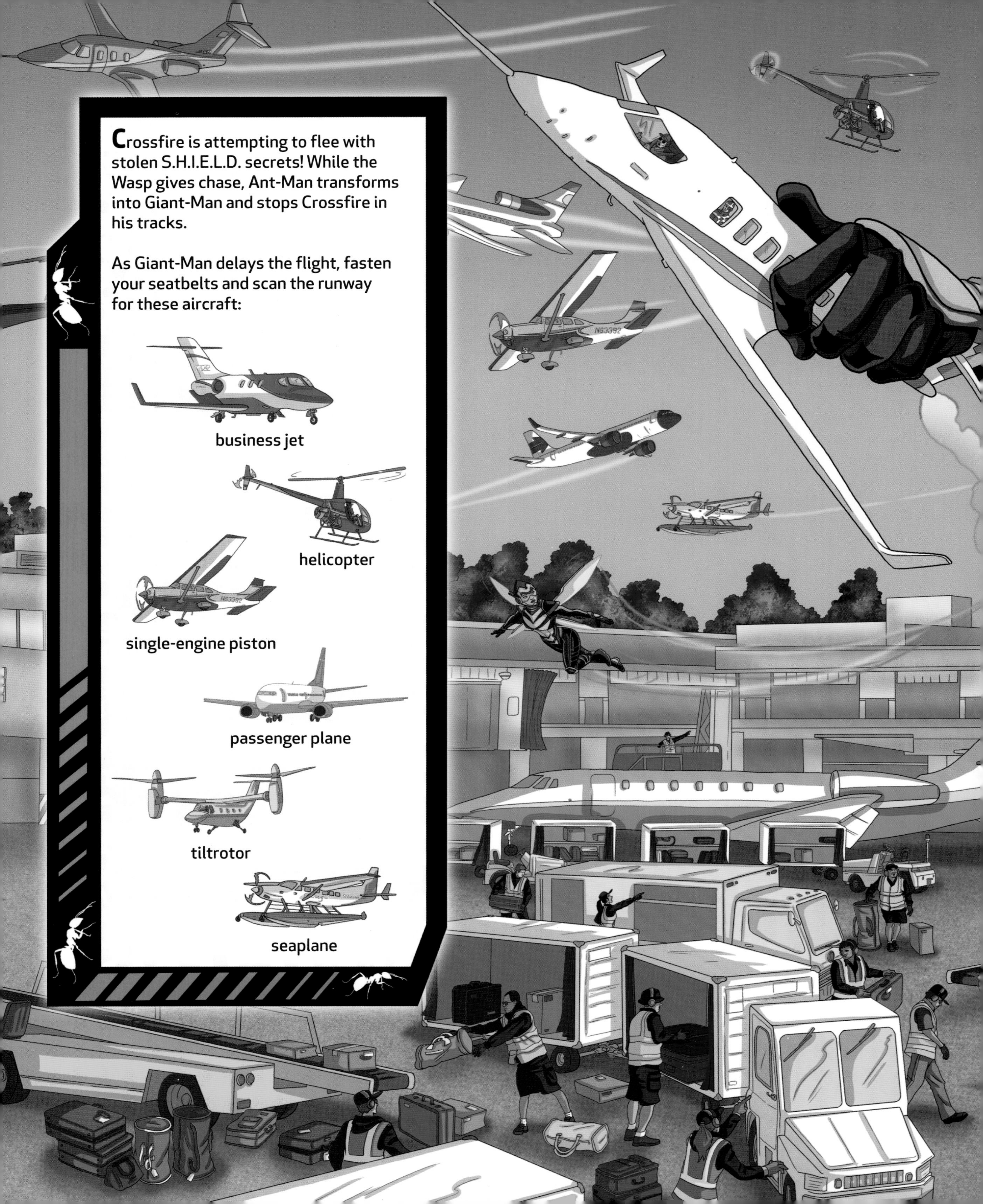

Crossfire is attempting to flee with stolen S.H.I.E.L.D. secrets! While the Wasp gives chase, Ant-Man transforms into Giant-Man and stops Crossfire in his tracks.

As Giant-Man delays the flight, fasten your seatbelts and scan the runway for these aircraft:

business jet

helicopter

single-engine piston

passenger plane

tiltrotor

seaplane

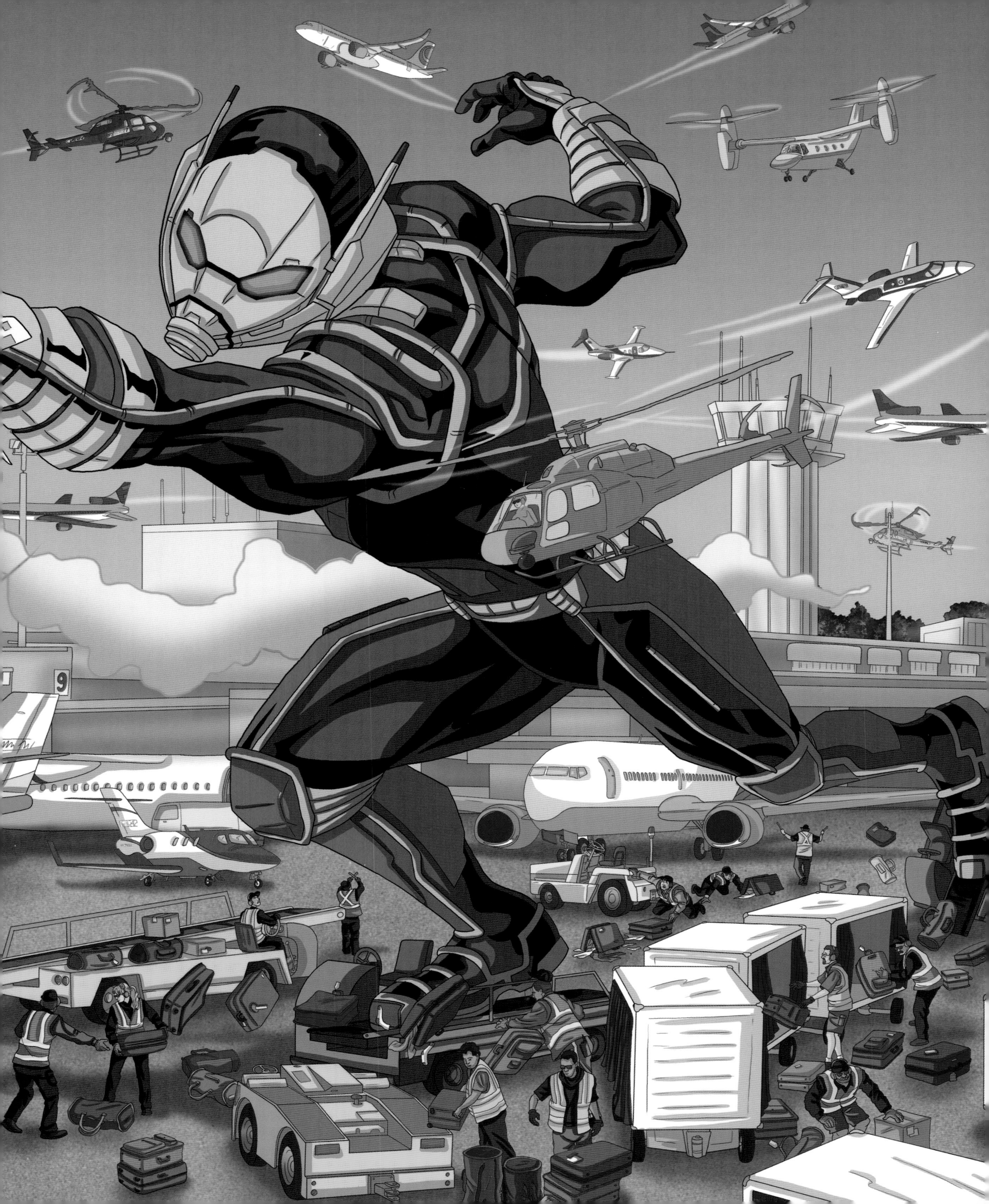
9

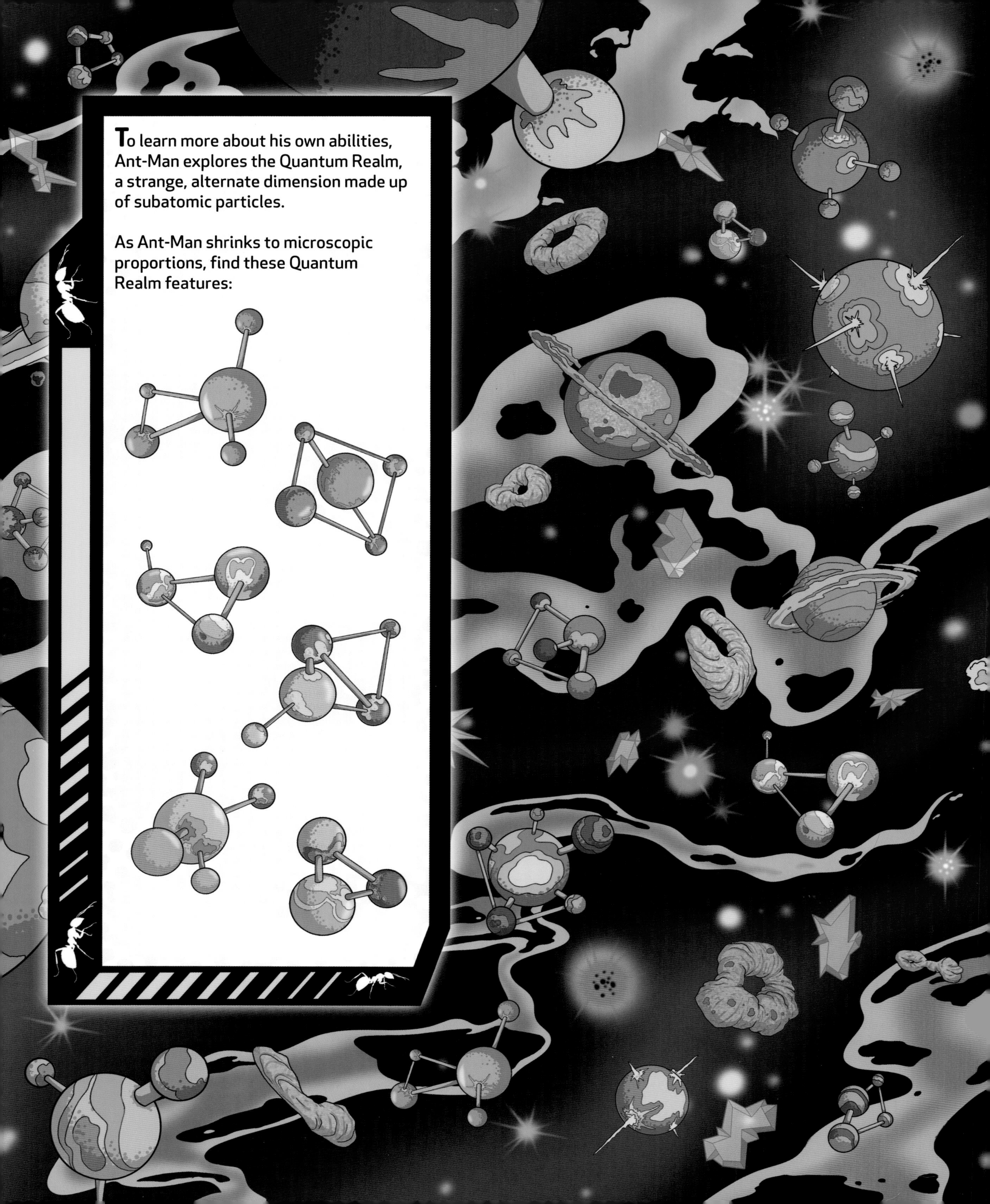

To learn more about his own abilities, Ant-Man explores the Quantum Realm, a strange, alternate dimension made up of subatomic particles.

As Ant-Man shrinks to microscopic proportions, find these Quantum Realm features:

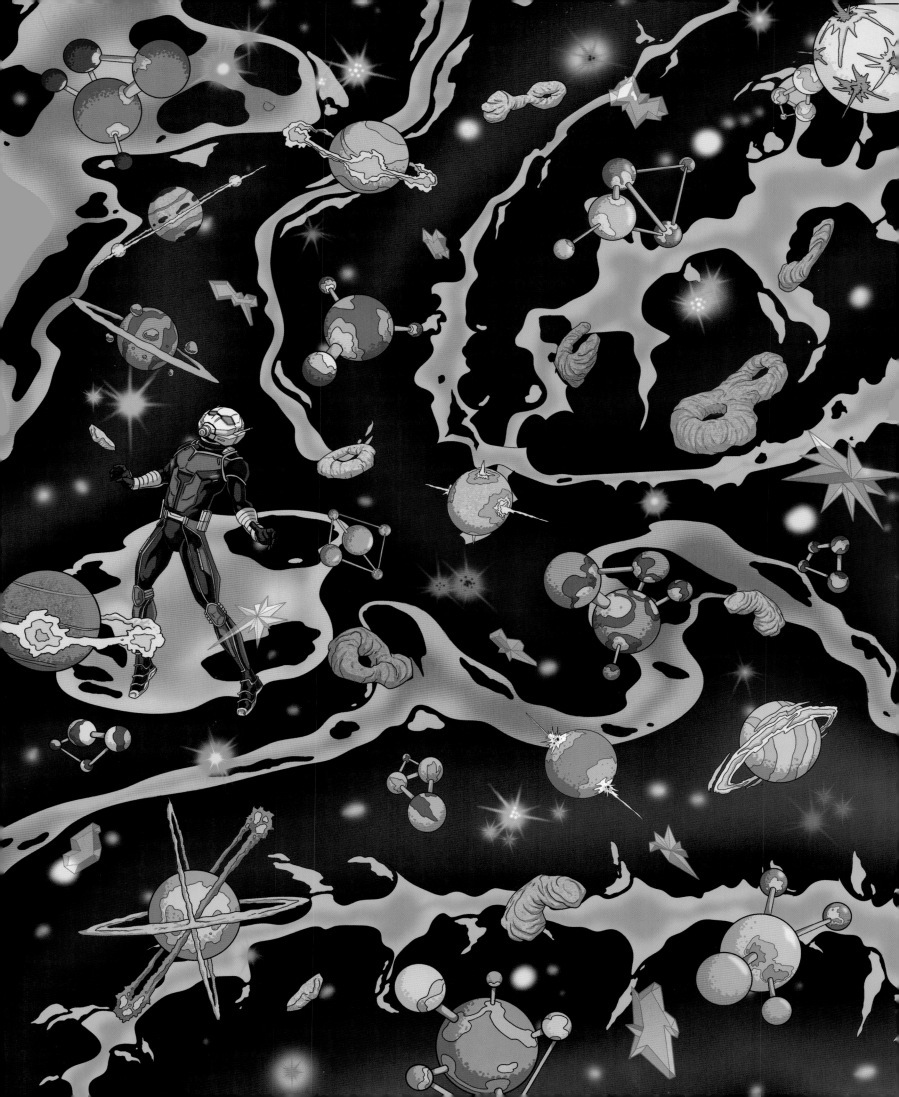

The Avengers hatch a plan to disrupt Hydra's headquarters! Ant-Man and the Wasp sabotage Hydra's clocks, sowing confusion and disarray throughout the compound.

While Ant-Man and the Wasp turn back time, look for these clock parts:

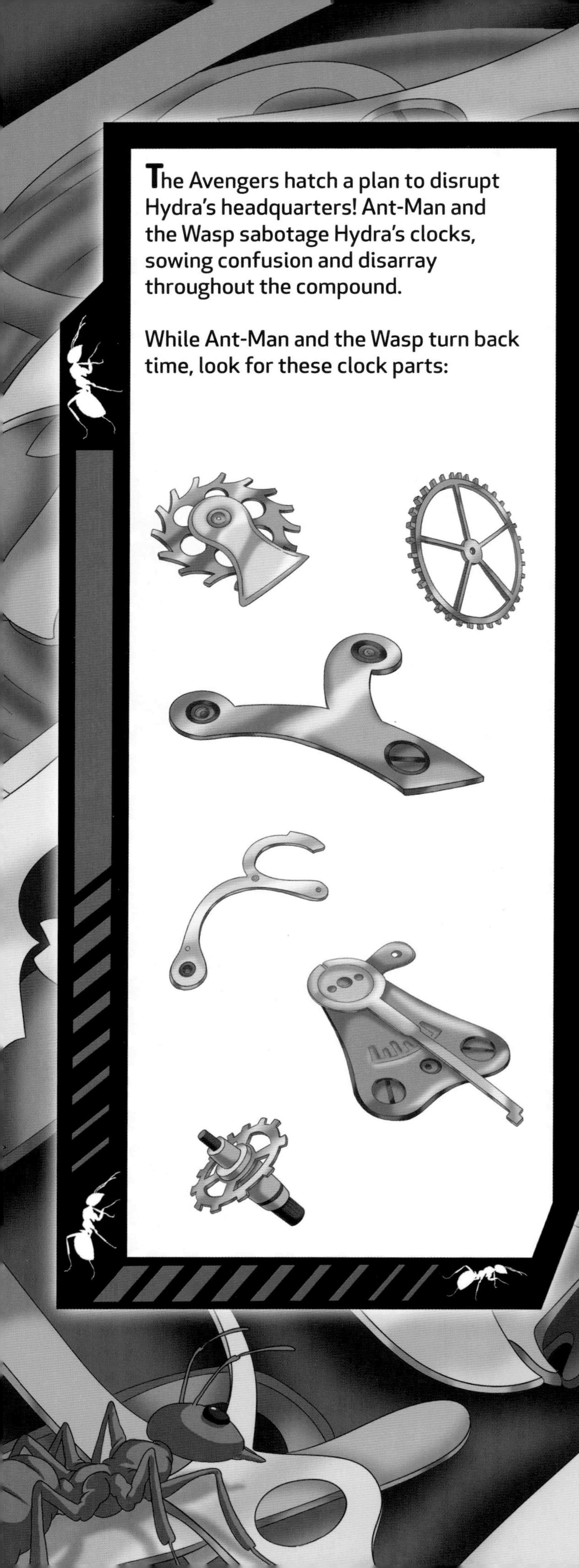

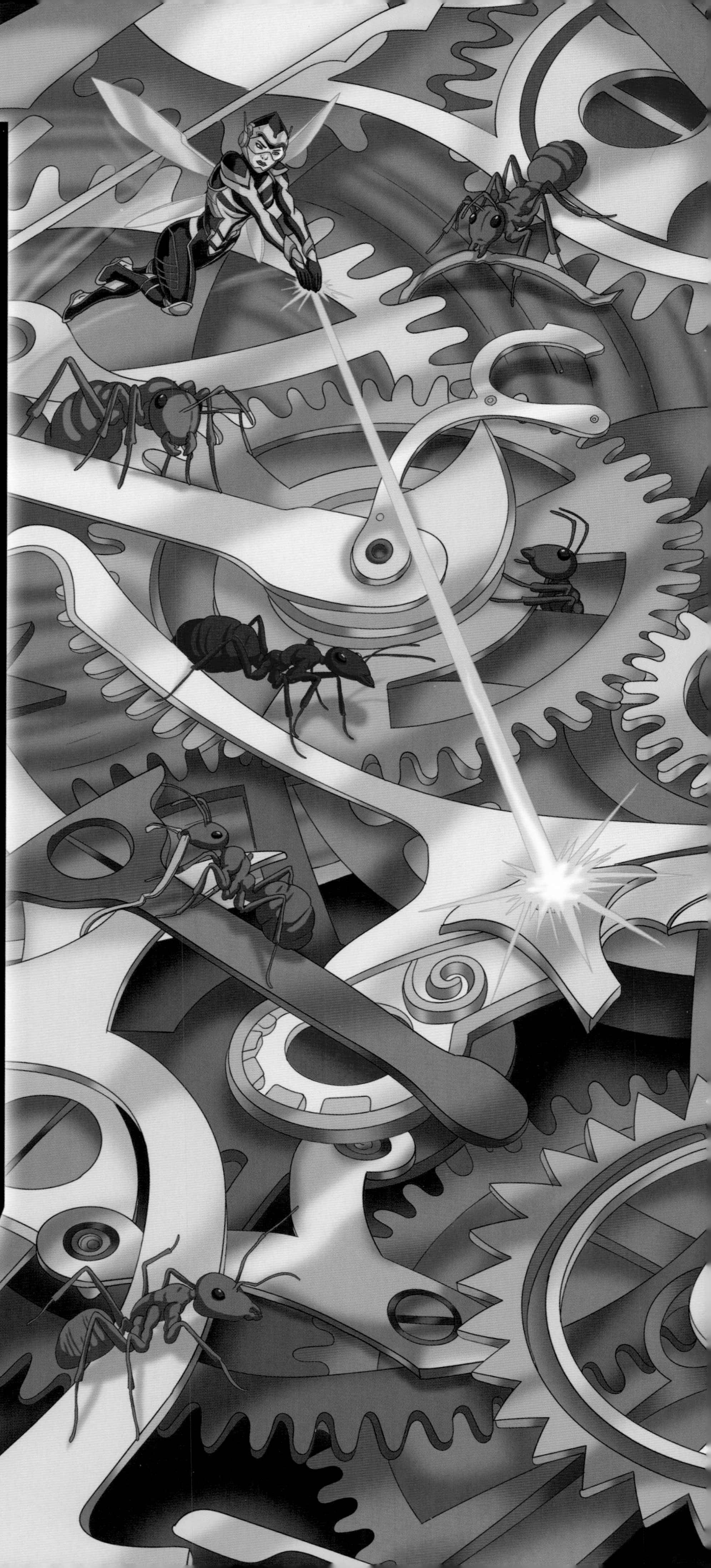

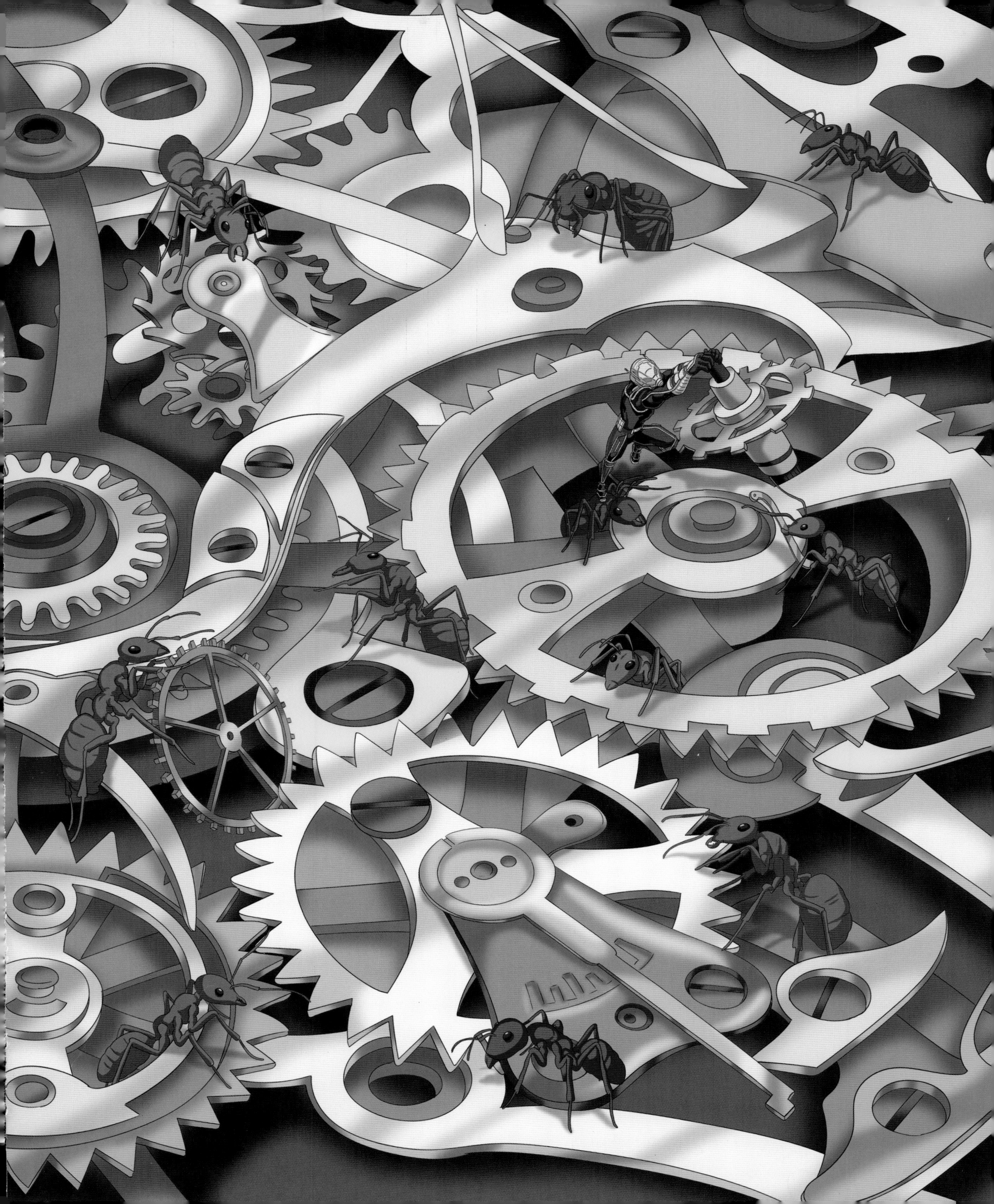

Leap back to Scott Lang's kitchen and find these household items:

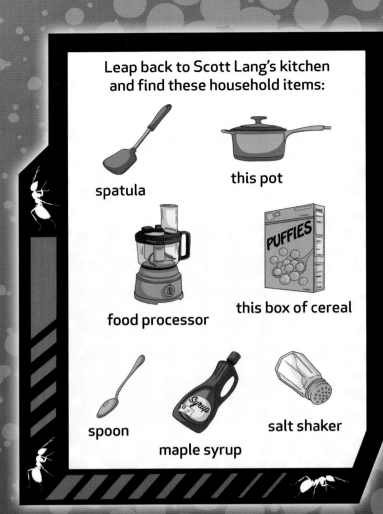

spatula
this pot
food processor
PUFFIES
this box of cereal
spoon
Syrup
maple syrup
salt shaker

Zip back to Zola's labyrinthine library and find these books:

HYDRA 101
How to Be FUN at Parties
GENOMES: The Splice of LIFE
Biochemistry
I Was a Teenage Bio-Fanatic

Along with his powers, Taskmaster has an arsenal of trick arrows. Hurry back to the battle and spot these:

March back to the magnifying glass and locate former S.H.I.E.L.D. agent Mitch Carson, along with these Hydra agents:

Please don't touch! Meander back to the museum and find these historical artifacts:

this figurine

carved elephant

this mask

statue

this clay pot

this model plane

this plate

Take a one-way flight back to the airport and find these bewildered baggage handlers:

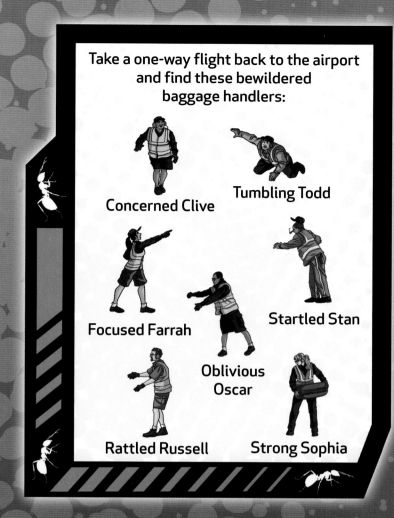

Concerned Clive

Tumbling Todd

Focused Farrah

Startled Stan

Oblivious Oscar

Rattled Russell

Strong Sophia

Mill about the Quantum Realm once more and find these subatomic asteroids:

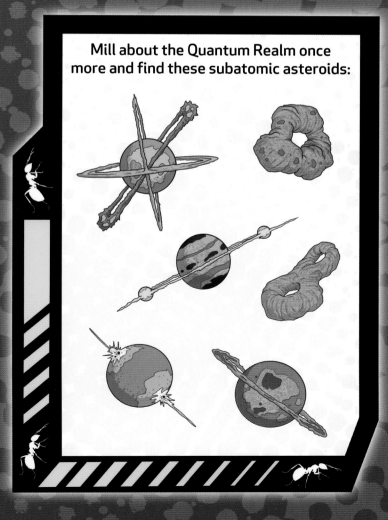

Climb back into the clock and count these cooperative ants:

ant running late

ant falling back

ant who is right twice a day

ant springing forward

ant working round-the-clock

punctual ant

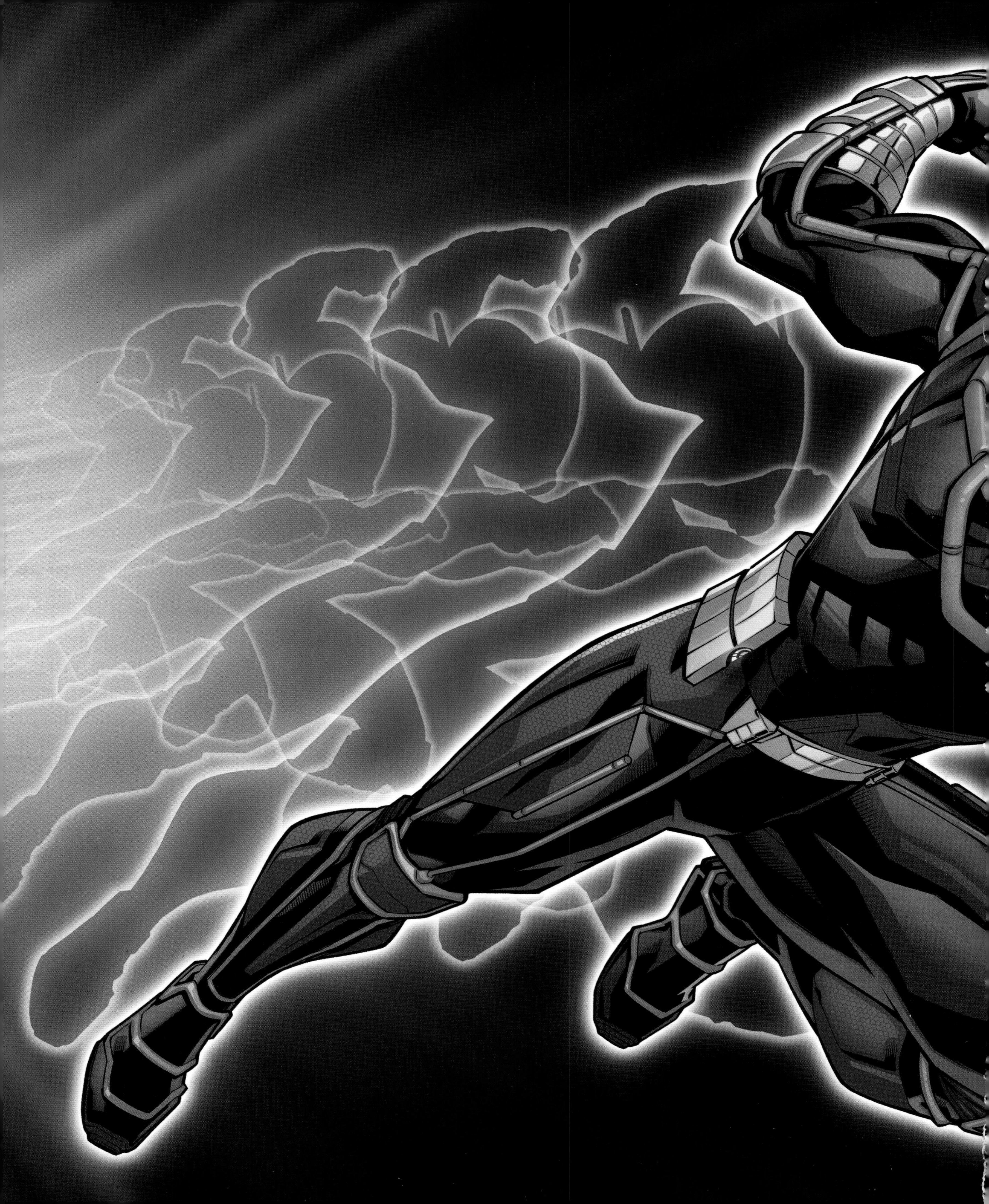